The Berenstain Bears and the REAL EASTER EGGS

To celebrate new life at Easter,
eggs and bunnies come in handy.
But some cubs think
it's just about candy.

A First Time Book®

EASTER EGG HUNT
HEADQUARTERS

Copyright © 2002 by Berenstain Enterprises, Inc. All rights reserved.
Published in the United States by Random House Children's Books,
a division of Random House, Inc., New York.
Random House and the colophon are registered trademarks of Random House, Inc.
First Time Books and the colophon are registered trademarks of Berenstain Enterprises, Inc.
randomhouse.com/kids
BerenstainBears.com
Library of Congress Cataloging-in-Publication Data
Berenstain, Stan. The Berenstain Bears and the real Easter eggs / by Stan & Jan Berenstain.
p. cm. — (A first time book)
Summary: The Berenstain Bear cubs are anxiously awaiting all the candy and Easter eggs that
Easter will bring, but Mama Bear and Mother Nature show them the true wonders of the season.
ISBN 978-0-375-81133-3 (trade) — ISBN 978-0-375-98247-7 (ebook)
[1. Easter—Fiction. 2. Bears—Fiction.] I. Berenstain, Jan. II. Title.
PZ7.B4483 Bejq 2002 [E]—dc21 2001041882
Printed in the United States of America 30 29 28 27 26 25 24 23 22

The Berenstain Bears and the REAL EASTER EGGS

Stan & Jan Berenstain

Random House · New York

". . . Nineteen . . . twenty . . . twenty-one . . . twenty-two . . . twenty-three. How about that?" said Sister Bear. "I got twenty-three valentines at school today—seven signed with names, eight guess-whos, and eight S.W.A.K.s."

Brother smiled. He knew that there were twenty-four cubs in Sister's class and Teacher Jane made every cub give every other cub a valentine.

But Sister was enjoying her valentines so much that he didn't say anything. Besides, he'd gotten quite a few himself.

"I just *love* holidays!" said Sister. "I wish every day was a holiday. Then you could get stuff every day."

"Oh?" said Mama, who'd been listening. "Is that all holidays mean to you—getting stuff?"

"Sure," said Sister. "You get turkey, stuffing, and pumpkin pie on Thanksgiving, presents on Christmas, and valentines on Valentine's Day. What's wrong with that?"

"What's *wrong* with that," said Mama, "is that holidays are about much more. Thanksgiving is about being thankful, Christmas is about good will and peace on earth, and Valentine's Day is about love and friendship."

"What do you think about that, my dear?" asked Papa. "Er, where did Sister go?" he said, looking around.

"She went into the kitchen," said Brother.

Which Sister had.

She'd gone into the kitchen to look at the calendar on the wall. She was looking ahead for holidays. She looked at the rest of February. There weren't any more big holidays in February.

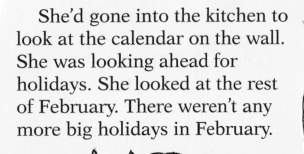

She looked at March. She didn't see any big holidays in March either.

But then she looked at April, and right there
in April was a really big holiday: *Easter! Yum!*
she thought. *Coconut eggs, jellybeans, chocolate
bunnies! Yum! And double yum!*

That night, Sister fell asleep while visions of jellybeans and chocolate bunnies danced in her head.

But it was still winter, and when she woke up the next morning she forgot about Easter and spring because there was a new blanket of snow covering the earth—

wonderful snow to sled on,

to make forts out of,

to make angel wings in.

But Mother Nature hadn't forgotten.

And while Brother, Sister, and their friends sledded and made forts and angel wings, she was getting ready for a whole new season.

As the winter winds died down and
the sun began to ride higher in the sky,
signs of spring began to appear.

The big icicles of winter dropped
from roofs and stuck like swords in
the last of the melting snow.

Robins began looking for
places to build their nests.

Blue and yellow
crocuses peeped through
the softening earth.

And it wasn't very long before reminders of Easter began to appear in supermarkets and

on television.

But it was the big billboard in the town square
that got Sister and Brother really excited about Easter.
This is what it said:

COMING SOON!
THE GIANT BEARTOWN
EASTER EGG HUNT!

DON'T MISS IT!

ALL CUBS WELCOME!

PRIZES! PRIZES! PRIZES!

• Delicious Chocolate Easter Eggs!
• Jellybeans! Jellybeans! Jellybeans!
• Gigantic Chocolate Bunnies!
• Every Cub Will Win A Prize!

All Prizes on display in window
of the Beartown General Store.

"Look," said Brother. "It says the prizes are on
display in the window of the Beartown General Store."

And were they ever!

There were more jellybeans than you could ever count; sugar-trimmed, dark-chocolate, coconut-filled eggs with sugar roses and violets on them; life-sized, milk-chocolate bunnies; and one chocolate bunny as big as Brother Bear himself.

Happy Easter, indeed! This was going to be the biggest, best, most delicious Easter ever.

GENERA

EASTER EGG
HUNT
PRIZES

Brother and Sister were so excited they ran all the way home.

Mama was in the tree house front yard.

"Sister," said Brother, "you tell Mama about the big Easter egg hunt while I go find Papa and tell him."

"Mama! Mama!" sputtered Sister. She was so excited and out of breath she could hardly talk.

"Now, my dear," said Mama, "I know that what you want to tell me is very exciting, but I'm sure it can wait until you catch your breath. Meanwhile, I've got some exciting things to show you."

"But, Mama!" protested Sister.

"Just look here," said Mama, kneeling down. "See these little blue and yellow flowers? They're from the crocus bulbs I planted last fall. They've been sleeping under the snow all winter. Now they're the first to push up through the earth and greet the spring. Aren't they lovely?"

"Yes, Mama, they're nice," said Sister. "But Brother and I were just down at the town square and guess what?"

But Mama didn't quite hear Sister because she had walked across the yard and was looking closely at a scratchy-looking bush. It didn't look like much to Sister.

"This is a forsythia," said Mama. "It doesn't look like much now, but come the first warm, sunny day it will burst with thousands of brilliant yellow flowers. Surely you remember it from last spring, my dear?"

Sister did, sort of. And it *was* pretty. But it didn't begin to compare with those sugar roses and violets on those dark-chocolate Easter eggs, or those zillions of brightly colored jellybeans.

That's when Papa and Brother came running around the house. Papa was just as excited as Brother and Sister.

"How about that?" cried Papa. "How about what?" said Mama. "Didn't Sister tell you?" said Papa. "There's going to be a big Easter egg hunt on the town square and you should hear the prizes—more jellybeans than you could ever count—"

"Papa?" said Brother.

"All kinds of chocolate eggs!" continued Papa.

"Papa?" repeated Brother, tugging on Papa's pants leg.

"Er, yes, son?"

"I forgot to tell you," said Brother. "The Easter egg hunt is just for cubs."

"Just for cubs?" said Papa.

"That's right," said Brother.

"Oh," said Papa. He was more than a little disappointed. Papa was crazy about jellybeans—especially the black ones.

Mama sighed. She looked at Papa and the cubs. She was a little disappointed, too.

The day of the Easter egg hunt dawned bright and early. Sister, Brother, and dozens of their friends were on the town square waiting for Mayor Honeypot to give the signal for the hunt to begin. They had bags and baskets of every shape to gather the eggs. Brother and Sister were especially well prepared. They each had a big basket—the better to carry the eggs they would find.

EASTER EGG HUNT
HEADQUARTERS

GENERAL STORE

When the mayor gave the signal, it was helter-skelter, gather-gather—here an egg, there an egg, everywhere an egg-egg. But Brother and Sister had a plan. Instead of hunting where the other cubs were, they quickly moved to the woods at the edge of the square.

"Here's a red one and a pink one and a green one!" shouted Sister as she popped the eggs into her basket.

"And here's an orange one and a yellow one and a lavender one!" cried Brother as he popped them into his basket.

A little while later, Brother noticed that Sister had become very quiet.

He turned and saw her standing ever so still, looking into some bushes.

"*And here,*" said Sister in a soft, hushed voice that Brother could hardly hear, "are five tiny blue eggs in a nest deep in the bushes." Ever so carefully and quietly, Brother moved into the bushes and looked over Sister's shoulder at *the real Easter eggs.*

And together they watched as, one by one, each tiny blue egg cracked open and a tiny, scraggly, wet baby robin struggled to climb out. From time to time, the mother or father robin came to the nest with food—worms and insects. They took turns putting the food in the wide-open beaks of the baby birds.

Brother and Sister watched
for a long time. They hardly
moved. It was as if they were
under a spell. It was the most
wonderful and amazing thing
they had ever seen.

They missed most of the Easter egg hunt. But since every cub got a prize, they got some goodies for the eggs they had already gathered—a few chocolate eggs, but mostly jellybeans, which they shared with Papa. They gave him the black ones.

Many of Sister and Brother's friends won the really big prizes. But that was okay. The sugar-trimmed chocolate eggs and the giant chocolate bunny would not only soon be gone, they would leave quite a few tummy aches behind.